THE
BEAUTIFUL RAT

THE
BEAUTIFUL RAT

written and illustrated by KAETHE ZEMACH

FOUR WINDS PRESS   NEW YORK

For all my family
and friends
with Love

Library of Congress Cataloging in Publication Data

Zemach, Kaethe.
   The beautiful rat.
   SUMMARY: Mr. and Mrs. Rat search for someone
very great to be their daughter's husband.
   [1. Marriage — Fiction. 2. Rats — Fiction]
I. Title.
PZ7.Z413Be   [E]
ISBN 0-590-07584-5

PUBLISHED BY FOUR WINDS PRESS
A DIVISION OF SCHOLASTIC MAGAZINES, INC., NEW YORK, N.Y.
COPYRIGHT © 1979 BY KAETHE ZEMACH
ALL RIGHTS RESERVED
PRINTED IN THE UNITED STATES OF AMERICA
LIBRARY OF CONGRESS CATALOG CARD NUMBER: 79-11752
1   2   3   4   5   83   82   81   80   79

JAN '80

M any years ago there lived in Japan a family of rats.

The father was a very proud rat. From the tip of his nose to the end of his tail, inside and out, he was glad to be a rat.

The mother was also proud, but she was not a satisfied rat. She thought that life was probably better outside in the big world.

These two rats had an only daughter whose name was Yoshiko. She was the most beautiful girl in the rat

world. Her fur was smooth and soft as velvet. Her teeth were sharp and pointed. She was famous for her running, and well known for her leaps.

The time came when the mother and father rat decided that it was time for Yoshiko to get married.

Father Rat wanted Yoshiko to marry a young gentleman rat. Mother Rat, on the other hand, thought Yoshiko was much too special to marry a rat and live her life in a rat hole.

Yoshiko didn't care one way or the other; she spent her time playing with her friends. Her best friend, Toshio, had long whiskers which almost swept the ground.

Mother and Father Rat just could not agree about
a husband for Yoshiko. Their arguments got worse
and worse.

One day when Mother Rat was more excited than usual she shouted, "My daughter is MUCH too beautiful and clever to marry a rat! She can have better. Reach for the stars!"

"All right," growled Father Rat, "offer her to the sun if you like. There's nothing greater than the sun."

"I will!" said Mother Rat.

The next day they got themselves ready and set out along the big road.

After a while they came to the place where the sun lived. Mother Rat stepped right up and called out, "Oh mighty king! Let me introduce you to our daughter Yoshiko! She is famous in the rat world for her beauty and intelligence, and so we are looking for a very great husband for her."

"I see," said the sun. "I am honored indeed. But I have no time to get married. If you want the greatest husband you should consider the cloud, who is so much stronger than I."

Just then a cloud swept by and covered up the
rays of the sun.

Mother Rat called out, "Great and mighty cloud! This is Yoshiko, our beautiful daughter. She is so clever and so beautiful we are looking for a very great husband for her."

"Well, I live in cold, dark places," said the cloud. "But if you're looking for a very great husband, why don't you consider the wind, who is so much stronger than I."

Suddenly the wind came rushing by, and blew the cloud to the other side of the sky.

The wind stopped by an old stone wall. When the rats had tumbled back down to earth, Mother Rat caught her breath and cried, "Oh, your majesty! Meet Yoshiko, our beautiful daughter! We are looking for someone very great to be her husband."

"Well," said the wind, "I spend all my time rushing around, so I wouldn't be a good husband for your daughter. But if you want a truly great husband, let me introduce my friend, this old stone wall, which stops me in my flight and will not let me by."

Hearing this, Yoshiko leapt a mighty leap and shouted, "No! Never! I will *not* marry this old stone wall!"

The wall's feelings were hurt. His voice was sad. "Well, that's all right," he said. "Why should you marry a wall when you could have a rat for a husband? Those fine animals with their sharp teeth can nibble holes right through me."

The rats were very surprised! Mother Rat was tickled pink and Father Rat was delighted. Yoshiko was very happy, and glad it turned out so well.

So the three rats turned around and went back home.

There was much celebration, and they all agreed that Yoshiko would be happiest marrying her best friend Toshio, whose whiskers almost swept the ground.

Three days later, everyone danced at Yoshiko's wedding.